Tirangil's Mercy

Baylee Alger

M&B Global Solutions Inc.
Green Bay, Wisconsin (USA)

Tirangil's Mercy

Cover design and artwork: Naveed Anjum
https://www.fiverr.com/design9creative

ISBN: 978-1-942731-53-5

Designed and published by:
M&B Global Solutions Inc.
Green Bay, Wisconsin (USA)

Dedication

This book is for my uncle, Michael P. Lund. While writing this book, I realized how similar I am to Jalhan. He went away from his family for some time and almost lost connection with them entirely. He got his chance to reconnect with his family.

I can't wait for my chance to reconnect with Uncle Mike. I miss you every day, Uncle Mike. I hope you'd be proud of me.

Contents

Chapter One

The western coast of Klagrond was starkly beautiful in the winter. A smattering of snow clung to the cliffs overlooking the Sea of Hiding. Off to the east, down a rise, and some thirty miles off, the majestic forest of Sarvenkor appeared as a snowy smudge at the edge of sight. The bare stone and flat plains were desolate but pure, and they reflected the feeble winter sunlight into beautiful patterns of silvery blue in the sea mist, thrown up by the mighty waves that crashed upon the cliffs hundreds of feet below.

Jalhan Okarrest noticed none of this as he rode northward, the sheer drop to the rocks below a mere ten feet to his left. The towers that gave the city of Seatower its name cast him in their shadow as he rode away. His horse, a great beast named Bay, snorted and huffed at the uneven stone of their path. Jalhan pulled his velvety cloak tighter about him as the wind picked up, and once again cursed himself for coming here. He had family out this way, in a little village up north. Harban's Barrow, he thought it was called, but couldn't quite remember. He had the map his sister had sent him, a few days of food, and his armor packed into his saddlebags. He just wanted to get there, rest in front of a fire, and perhaps beneath the blankets with a local girl. He may have been a priest, but he was no prude.

Jalhan was truly imposing when dressed in his full silver plate. But for now, he simply wore a woolen tunic and breeches, along with his black cloak and boots.

He shivered once more, unable to shrink away from the wind. He pulled the cloak tighter, the hood higher, and tried his best to live with it.

He spurred Bay into a trot, and the animal huffed in indignation. He was always doing that. A horse as ornery as his master. They rode for hours without event, the roar of the wind on his face and the waves far below mixing into a dull, strangely comforting roar. Jalhan passed the time by counting birds, watching ships on the water, and dozing. He cursed himself, which he found himself doing plenty on this trip, for not bringing a book, although he knew his fingers would have frozen solid if he had.

So, he sat. And he sat. And he sat some more. He watched the sun rise and set. He slept. He ate. He did his business. He prayed to Tirangil. He began his travels anew. It took him three days of light riding along the coast to reach the village.

He pulled Bay to a stop on the hill overlooking the place. It was just another hamlet, one like many he'd traveled through in his wandering days. Larger than most with perhaps fifty buildings, mostly houses. A tavern, of course. A temple. A toy store, a general store, and an apothecary lined up on one street, a few eating establishments on another. He supposed hamlet wasn't the right word for the place. It was a large village, with a population of roughly two hundred. His sister, Halana, had built herself a life here. He was proud of her for that, though he wouldn't let her know it. Not right away at least. First, he needed to berate her for making him ride this damn far.

He climbed back into the saddle and rode down the hill toward the village. It was still a few miles off, and he knew he had another hour or so of riding before him. That was okay. The destination was in sight and that was all that mattered.

Jalhan rode into town around dusk, the sun sinking into the sea to the west as Elokar crept its way into the sky. He tied Bay outside an inn, a hardy building called The Year Round Icicle, and stepped through the doors. Sound, heat, and the smell of tobacco smoke hit him as he walked inside. The room was open, with the wooden ceiling beams lost in clouds of pipe smoke. The scent of brewing coffee, stew, meat, and Adinlei cakes filled the air as men and women sat chatting and laughing. A young man in bright colors picked at a lute on the small stage at one end of the room, but the cacophony mostly drowned out his music.

Jalhan doffed his cloak, hanging it upon the deer head coat rack beside the door, and walked across the room. He'd left his sword, the great slab of steel he was almost never without, outside with Bay. He kept his knife hidden in one of his black leather boots just in case, though he didn't think he'd need it.

Jalhan moved up to the bar, squeezing in beside a dwarf man, deep in the Adinlei wine, and a comely elf woman, who was polishing a dagger. He vaguely recognized her. Long red hair, lithe, yet curvy figure, and blue eyes. Laokis, he thought her name was. He turned to face her, a smile coming to his lips, and the woman didn't even give him a chance to speak.

"No. Not again," she said, pointing the dagger at him meaningfully.

"Aye, my lady," he said defensively, putting his hands up and turning back to the bar.

"Come now, Halana," he called out to the bartender. "Get me a drink."

"Oh you wait your turn," replied the barkeep, a plump woman in her mid-forties with more gray in her blond hair than he remembered. "Ahh yes, I forgot," he said. "The oldest always gets her way."

Halana turned and her eyes settled upon him. Her chubby face lit up, and she rushed around the bar to hug him. Jalhan hugged her tightly in return, then pushed her back to arm's length.

"The inn not been good to you?" he asked.

"Oh, quite the opposite," she said, disengaging from his grip. "And I'll have you know I never got my way with mother; you always got the attention."

"Yes, yes, a bartender must lie to get her tips. But I'm your brother, you needn't lie to me."

She scoffed, and the jovial reunion was quickly forgotten as they fell back into the familiar sibling squabbles.

"How's Hormas?" Jalhan asked as Halana poured him a glass of her finest Pinecrest whiskey, a favorite of his.

"Fine," she said. "He's at home with the children."

"Children? So, Kesa's a big sister now?"

"Aye, for four years now. You really ought to visit more, Jally."

He bristled at that. He hated that nickname, and she knew it. She noticed his discomfort and laughed with a sound that filled the room as it always had.

"I'm sorry," she said between barks of laughter. "I've forgotten you're the big, serious priest now. Not my little Jally."

She reached across the bar and pinched his cheek, and he lightly slapped her hand away, taking a pull of whiskey. The elf maid beside him, still polishing her dagger, chuckled to herself and Jalhan's face turned crimson.

He drained his glass and Halana poured him a refill.

"What's the second's name?" he asked, trying to pick

up the shreds of his dignity.

"Jalhan," she said. "He deserved a name he could be proud of."

Jalhan sat back on the stool, struck suddenly with guilt. He did his best not to show it outwardly, but he knew he failed. He hadn't been the best of siblings to Halana since their mother had died, a victim of some devious cancer. Their father had left years before and gotten himself killed in some foolish business venture. Something about mining gold in the Stormshatter Mountains, if memory served. He had been just eighteen, a young priest headed for Kuloran to begin his training, when he'd lost his mother. He'd thrown himself into his studies and ignored his older sister, who had taken the loss hard, harder than even he had. She'd left Pinecrest and came here, and he'd trained with blade and spell.

Priests were usually taught to speak directly to their chosen gods, and the results were miraculous. Jalhan called it magic. Others might call it luck. He'd trained in the blade at the academy of Kulor with the paladins.

Priests of Tirangil, like himself, were given the choice, and Jalhan had taken it immediately. It was another thing to distract him, to keep him from thinking about what really should have mattered to him then. In all of that time, he'd become something like his father. Always calm. Always cool. Always closed off. He could feel those barriers being broken now. It struck him how quickly good whiskey and better company had done it.

"I'm sorry, Hal," he said, and he meant it. "It's such a long trip and I just … I'm …"

"I know," she said simply, and patted his hand.

Clearing his throat, he took another drink of his whiskey. The dwarf beside him had fallen asleep and was snoring loudly, and the elf woman was now nursing a glass of wine, her knife nowhere to be seen. Jalhan couldn't help but notice her eyes trailing over to him, then flicking away just before she thought he'd notice. He was a striking figure by most accounts. Tall, just north of six feet, and heavily muscled, with a noble face, the cool, but not unkind, brown eyes of his father, and his mother's thick black hair. He usually wore heavy silver plate and a huge greatsword under his black cloak, but now he wore a simple tunic and breaches, with a knife in his leather boot.

"Have we plans for tomorrow?" he asked Halana when she came back around. "Dinner, perhaps?"

"Hormas has outdone himself," she said. "He's caught the biggest boar I've ever seen. You enjoyed his bacon last time you were here, didn't you?"

"Aye," Jalhan replied, taking a sip of whiskey. "Is he brewing again?"

"No, thank Eludora," she said with a nervous chuckle. "He never could get the wine to not taste like fermented piss. You might like it, though. I think we still have some."

"No, no thank you," he said, as he drained his glass. The alcohol filled his body with a pleasant warmth, one that shielded him from the blasts of cold air as people came and went.

Halana laughed and turned to the room. "Last call, folks!" she shouted. "I got a family to cook for tomorrow, and I know most of you have wives waiting. Especially you, Garald."

A fat man in a too tight friar's robe groaned as the pretty young woman sitting on his lap turned and slapped him before scampering off.

"Shame on you," Halana said, poking a pudgy finger in his direction before turning her attention to the influx of men and women calling for their last drinks. As she set about closing tabs and shooing people away, Jalhan turned to the elf woman beside him again.

"So. Can we try this again?" he asked, looking her up and down.

"We can," she said, a playful glint in her eye. "Though if you ask me to call you Jally in bed, I'll still kill you."

"Well then," he said, standing up. "You've changed your mind quickly."

The elf shrugged. "It's cold. I have needs, too."

Halana sighed from the other side of the bar. "Don't be late," she said to Jalhan, without even turning around. "And Laokis, if you must kill him, wait until after dinner tomorrow. Hormas cooked for five, and he wouldn't want to waste food."

"No promises," Laokis said, dragging Jalhan away by the hand. He found himself quite full of holiday spirit at that moment.

Chapter Two

Jalhan woke, tangled in sheets and limbs. He lay on Laokis's soft feather mattress, the beautiful elf woman lying with her legs intertwined with his, her bare back pressed into his chest. His arm rested beneath hers, and despite remembering most of what had happened last night, he couldn't suppress a blush as he lightly pulled his hand from her breast.

Carefully, he disentangled himself, rose, and walked across the creaky wooden floor to the wash closet. He answered nature's call and returned to find the red-headed elf sitting up, drinking from a cup of water she kept on her bedside table.

"Good morning," he said, sitting beside her on the bed. "Happy Adin's Day."

"Is it?" she asked, rubbing her forehead. "I feel as though I've been kicked by a horse. Above, below, all over." She gave him a teasing smile, which was somewhat diminished by her obvious hangover.

Laokis too rose and moved to her wash closet. She returned shortly after, and by this time Jalhan had dressed. He was lacing up his boots as she walked back into the room.

"Leaving so soon?" she asked, sounding somewhat disappointed. Though, he had to admit to himself, there was a good chance she was just being polite.

"I'm late as it is," he said, his joints cracking as he stood. He rubbed the remainder of the sleep from his eyes as he went for his cloak. "Halana will be expecting me, and that woman angry is the one thing that truly scares me in this world."

"She's just smart," Laokis said, as she too dressed.

"Maybe."

Jalhan pulled his cloak over his shoulders and stepped out of her bedroom. Laokis owned a small home on the edge of town, a two-room affair with a living space and kitchen in one half and her bedroom in the other. He could hear the sound of the waves over the brisk wind outside, and a brief memory returned of slipping in the sand on the way to her home.

"Care to walk with me?" he asked Laokis as she entered the room, dressed in a fresh tunic and breeches, still barefoot.

"No," she said, moving over to her kitchen area. "I need coffee. Then I have things to do."

"Nobody to meet for dinner?"

Laokis sighed. "Jalhan, we're not spouses. We were lovers for the night and that's all. You needn't concern yourself with the deeper aspects of my life."

"Fair enough," he said, hiding the pang of hurt he felt at her words. He liked to think of himself as an unshakable wall, but a beautiful woman was the strongest of winds for him. "I'll be off, then," and left without another word.

Harban's Barrow was quiet at this time of day. The small village was situated along the coast of the Sea of Hiding. The high cliffs Jalhan had rode along gradually sloped down until they no longer existed. Now, there was only the wide, flat beach, and Laokis's home was set at the beginning of the sand. Sea mist swirled around the house, and he had to take a moment to orient himself. The ocean was still a few hundred yards off, yet the icy winds hit Jalhan like a hammer.

He'd stabled Bay the night before. As pretty as Laokis was, his horse was his companion. So, he'd made her wait, and left the horse and his belongings to be kept by the stable master. He set out that way, walking between high banks of snow piled up against the sparse trees that grew beside the beach. Halana lived near the stables, so he'd check on her first, mostly to avoid her wrath, and then tend his horse.

As he walked, Jalhan found his mind drifting back over the years. His family hadn't been wealthy, but they had been comfortable, and they'd taken a vacation or two in their days. Jalhan could only remember one, though. His father had wanted his children to see how people outside of Pinecrest lived. They'd packed for months of travel and headed down through Sarvenkor and east to Rendgarde. Jalhan had found this thrilling, seeing the sights of the mighty trees of Sarvenkor, meeting people who spent their days living and working in the fields.

There was one village he would never forget: Greypatch. He and his family had spent a few days there, helping the farmers and tending to the sick. It was much like Harban's Barrow, if not in size, in hardiness. The people there lived in wooden houses and walked on dirt streets, but they were happy, healthy, and content. It had a lot of culture to it. Jalhan had met an old man there, a priest of

Tirangil named Hivoram. Jalhan had snuck away from his family, just a mischievous seven-year-old, and gotten lost in the graveyard north of the little village. He'd been afraid, unnerved by the tombstones and death around him. Then, a kind old man stepped out of the shadows and took him in. He taught Jalhan of the ways of Tirangil, at least in the little time he'd had.

Jalhan's parents found them later, drinking tea in the little chapel. Jalhan remembered that moment. He'd felt big in a way he hadn't before. Respected. His father had ruined all of that, storming in and admonishing him. As he dragged Jalhan toward the door, Hivoram slipped his holy symbol into Jalhan's hand. He'd kept that treasure his entire life. In some ways, he remembered that old man he'd known for but an hour as more of a father than his own had ever been. The following year, when his father left on his expedition for gold, Jalhan felt nothing. He felt nothing when he realized his father would never return. All he could remember was the kindness of an old man he barely knew, and the pained look in his mother's eyes as she watched her husband break that bond. At least, the physical one.

Jalhan shook himself back to the present. He'd need to make a point to visit Hivoram someday when he could. But now, he had to be on his way.

Something immediately struck Jalhan as the first businesses came into view. It was Adin's Day, he supposed, but none of the shops looked open. There were no lights in the windows of the homes built around or above them. The happy murmur of children opening their gifts didn't fill the air. The sea mist he'd been faced with at Laokis's home hadn't abated even a mile or so inland. It also felt different. Heavier on his skin, muting everything around him like a soft, but damp blanket. The air still smelled of the sea, snow, and the fleeting remnants of dying cookfires. Even the wind, though blowing strongly off the sea, felt diminished, less cutting, and more like a muted hammer blow in the background.

Jalhan shrugged. Perhaps they were sleeping in. All the same, he placed his hand on the pommel of his dagger, loosening it in its sheath. He headed down the main thoroughfare, his boots crunching in a fresh blanket of soft snow and occasionally clicking on the cobbles beneath. Harban's Barrow really was beautiful, he had to admit. He'd traveled through enough hamlets in the early days of his training, when priests were taught to work their miracles on the poor and the sick, and he'd seen the absolute worst rural Klagrond had to offer. Dirt, shit, squalor. He'd done his best to alleviate as much of that for the people he encountered as he could, but he was just one priest. Harban's Barrow was like none of those.

The sturdy stone and brick buildings on either side of the road were kept up nicely. The rooftops were shingled in slate and every one of the windows in the little town was glass. The taverns weren't dens for depravity, they were meeting houses for the hard-working, hardy folk of this place.

He passed a toy store, its front windows full of wooden dolls, metal Gnomish contraptions, and a stuffed bear about as tall as Jalhan. He found that one somewhat unnerving, its big glass eyes blank and staring. He suppressed a shudder and moved on.

Jalhan arrived at Halana's about twenty minutes later. He climbed her front steps, stomping his boots off on the straw mat she kept on the wooden deck. He raised a hand to knock and waited. Nothing. Not even a creak of floorboards. He knocked again, this time a little louder. Still nothing.

The mist swirled about him as he stood on the wooden planks, worry starting to eat its way into his mind. Had Halana been hurt? The children?

"Halana!" he shouted, pounding on the door full strength now.

Still nothing. The mist continued to swirl about him.

"Jalhan," he heard, a whisper just beside his right ear. Drawing his knife, he spun, punching out with his free hand. His fist passed through thin air. Nobody was there. He turned back to the door, and suddenly lurched as a tendril of mist wrapped around his chest, pulling him backward off the porch. He fell flat on his back, winded, and pushed himself to his feet. He retrieved his knife from a snowbank and stood, heart racing as he brandished the blade. The mist swirled. It did not attack again.

Jalhan felt his anger surging. Something was wrong here, very wrong. Someone was trying to keep him from his sister. He strode up the porch steps and kicked the door down with one adrenaline-fueled kick. He charged into the interior, knife drawn, expecting some assailant to be waiting there.

There was no one. The house was still. Silent. He stepped through the small front room of his sister's home, one of the larger, multi-room houses in the Barrow, and entered the kitchen. A meal sat on the table, unfinished. The chairs were pushed in neatly, silverware set atop the plates, some still with bits of now-cold food upon them. A simple dinner. A dinner from the night before, perhaps a late one.

Jalhan was on edge now. He drew his dagger, the six-inch steel blade comforting in his grip. He walked, slowly, into the living space, the cushioned chairs facing the fireplace in a neat row. That was Halana's way. Neat, tidy, and always spotless. There were no signs of a struggle, but there were no signs of Halana or her family either.

"Hally? Kesa?" he called out. He heard nothing except the wind outside.

He slowly climbed the staircase to the second floor of the home, passing the open doors of the children's bedrooms. He stepped into Kesa's, gazing around the room. It was utterly normal for a seven-year-old girl. Wooden horses, pink painted walls, a bed with a pink duvet, and a stuffed bear.

The bear was curious. Unless she'd grown out of it, which Jalhan assumed she hadn't given its presence, Kesa never went anywhere without that bear. She'd named him Pawsome, for reasons Jalhan never learned. He reached down and picked it up. A pain shot through him then, a pain so deep and profound that he found himself sitting on the small bed. He had missed out on so much. His own bravado and anger and grief had kept him from his sister for so long. His niece and nephew hardly knew him. They were strangers to him. And now ... Now he had no clue where they could be. He set Pawsome down and slid off the bed, kneeling in the center of the room to pray.

The rest of the home was much the same. Everything was where it should be. Little Jalhan's room was a mess, though he guessed that was just the perpetual state of a four-year-old boy's room. The master bedroom gave him a single clue: The bed was unmade. That was unheard of in Halana's household.

Jalhan was more unnerved than ever and left the house. He felt naked and exposed. He needed his armor and blade. He quickly walked to the stable, cursing aloud as he passed through the big barn doors. The stable was empty. Each and every stall was open, chain locks swinging as he passed. Bay's stall was empty and his saddlebags were gone. Jalhan kicked the stall door in anger. He stood in the center of the large room, fighting for his composure. He needed to focus. He needed to get to the bottom of this. He stood, breathing slowly, deeply. Calming himself. The scent of horseflesh and clean hay still pervaded the room. He could see sacks of apples and sugar cubes, carrots and other feed stacked in the corners. It was so normal, so mundane, he felt almost foolish. A tendril of mist wormed its way across the floor through a crack in the barn doors, writhing unnaturally toward him. Jalhan paid it no mind. He stood, clutching his holy symbol. Tirangil was with him. Tirangil would guide him. He had to know that.

By the time Jalhan turned back around, the mist had retreated. He walked back out into the blustery morning air. The mist and fog had thickened at an alarming rate, and he could only see by the feeble rays of winter sunlight that were strong enough to penetrate it. He stood in front of the stables and considered his next move. He'd have to sweep the village for clues. He vowed to enter every business, every home, every tavern, and restaurant and shop to find where everyone had gone. He ran his cold hands over his face, and he set out into town.

The first place he went was, of course, The Year Round Icicle. The wooden icicle above its door swayed in the wind, clunking dully against the wooden siding. The door was locked, as he'd expected, but a little jimmying with his dagger and the door opened easily. The interior was dark and cold, utterly alien compared to the night before. The tables were washed with chairs neatly set upon them, and not a single speck of dust swirled in the wind coming through the door. Mist followed him in as he shut the door, and it seemed to quickly rush into every corner, attaching itself there. Jalhan slowly moved to the central hearth, looking down at the polished flagstones at its base. Not a scuff. Not a clue. Nothing.

He took the poker set beside the fireplace, weighing it in his hands. It was iron and not built for fighting. But he would need something to defend himself that wasn't his knife. He hadn't fought with a spear in many years, not since his training days. But he remembered enough of the craft to feel confident.

Jalhan turned to leave, but paused. Something was

out of place here. His eyes cast about the room, searching, until he heard the same sound that had tipped him off before. The scuffing of leather on wood. But where was it coming from?

He turned, calmly, listening. There it was again, from the opposite direction. He spun, quickly, lashing out with the poker, and it sank into flesh. Into Halana's flesh.

"No," he breathed, as he looked upon his sister, impaled on his poker. "No, no, no."

His heart stopped. His fingers went numb. The poker came free from his hands, but did not fall, lodged as it was in Halana's chest. He stumbled toward her, catching her as she began to topple.

"Hally," he breathed.

His sister's eyes focused on him. No ... these were not Halana's eyes. These eyes were cold. Hateful. Grey. A clawed hand shot up, grasping him by the throat, and the thing that wasn't Halana lurched up toward him, teeth bared. Grey teeth. Grey eyes. Grey flesh. He drew his dagger and drove it savagely up through the thing's chin.

But it just kept coming. The thing pushed him roughly to his back, straddling him, both clawed hands upon his throat. Jalhan kept stabbing, ineffectually. He slashed the creature's wrists, which turned to mist and formed again, unharmed. He was beginning to black out ... He was going to fail ...

This can't be real, he told himself, and suddenly, it wasn't. He lay on his back. His throat ached and the poker had clattered loudly to the floor beside him. But the creature was no longer there. Just swirling mist.

Jalhan rolled over, pushing himself up as he coughed. He spat into the cold hearth and picked up his weapons, leaning on the old iron poker for support. He stumbled out of the tavern into a world that had gone black. The fog and mist had rolled in off the sea, or wherever accursed place it had come from, and he couldn't see a thing. He fumbled in his breeches, finding a match. Stepping back inside, took a taper off the wall and lit it, and just like that the fog and mist retreated, almost hissing. He felt a hand on his shoulder then and he spun, swinging with his poker.

A leather-clad form rolled backward, arms coming up to block his strike.

"Jalhan!" it shouted, the voice familiar. But Jalhan was on his guard now, and he followed as the form lurched backward. It drew a blade, a long, thin sword that parried his next attack. "Lekyros damn it, Jalhan, it's me!"

Jalhan stopped dead.

"Laokis?" he asked, letting the point of the poker drop into the snow. "Is that you?"

"Yes," she said, and the rasp of steel on leather told him she'd put her blade away. He approached her through the mist, which, though clearer, still blanketed the world in grey.

He pulled the woman close, hugging her tightly, letting himself relax for a brief moment. Laokis, surprised by the sudden affection, squeezed him. He was shaking. He was afraid. He was angry and he was worried. These were all emotions he was not used to feeling. These were all emotions he'd tried to put out of himself years ago, and clearly that effort was to little success. He was just a scared little boy in a world he didn't understand. And that fact enraged him.

Abruptly, Jalhan stepped out of her arms and turned.

"We have more places to investigate," he said, brushing an unshed tear from his eye. "We stick together. The mist will try to play tricks on your mind. Resist them."

He strode off into the snow and mist, Laokis trailing behind him. He couldn't see the worry on her face. He wouldn't have cared if he could.

They spent the next few hours searching through the various houses of the town, and Jalhan felt a new spike of pain with each one. Families he could have known. Friends he could have made. Their lives, all laid out before him; a book he wished he'd read.

The houses bore no fruit, though, and the pair stood, exhausted, in the center of the main street. It had already been a long, long day. They were hot despite the freezing gale. They were tired. They were hungry, and they were defeated.

They returned to Laokis's home and shared a midafternoon meal. As they sat, eating a roast chicken Laokis had been saving for her quiet Adinlei dinner, Jalhan set down his knife.

"Do you have any regrets, Laokis?"

The woman seemed taken aback by the question.

"What?" she asked, unable to formulate any other response.

"Regrets," he repeated, "Do you have any?"

He saw her face tighten. Her eyes flashed with anger. He saw the exact moment she retreated into herself.

"We should be going soon," Laokis said, rising from the table.

She brought her dishes to a basin of hot, soapy water and dumped them in, brushing her hands off on a roughspun towel.

Jalhan sighed. This day was certainly teaching him things. He was letting his emotions win. He wasn't sure why. This had never been like him. But they were winning and he was losing, and he had to do something about it. He closed his eyes. He breathed deeply. He pushed the worries from his mind. He pushed the terror he felt at the potential loss of his sister, his brother-in-law, his niece, and his nephew to a small corner of his mind. He pushed the regrets he felt for the lack of connection he had with them and the residents of this beautiful little town into another. He fought down the anger he felt at feeling these things. He was a priest of Tirangil, gifted in blade and strong in magic. He wouldn't allow himself this weakness again.

He laughed to himself, bitterly. He had to admit that if he really bought that, he was a greater fool than he already thought he was.

They forged back into the snow about ten minutes later. Jalhan wore a spare sword across his back, one a great deal shorter and thinner than he was used to. Laokis had informed him that she had been an Okanrelian Royal Hunter for some time, and she did well to have spares of all of her weapons. He wore one of those now, and it was a great deal more effective than his dagger. They walked in silence, the sound of their boots in the snow and the crashing of the waves strangely muted. Jalhan thought it almost ethereal.

"Stop," Laokis said, and he stopped. They were facing the toy store now, the red brick building a chilling specter in the cloying mist. "Something's different."

She was right.

"The bear," he murmured. "It's not there."

Laokis nodded, and the pair drew their swords in tandem. They approached the big glass doors at the front of the building, and they were, strangely, unlocked.

The silver bell above the doors rang pleasantly, despite their best efforts to keep it quiet. The sound was like a thunderclap in the cavernous space within. The toy store was one of the largest buildings in town. Halana had told him once that it was a repurposed warehouse. The smell of wood and fish still clung to the air, though faintly, a distant echo of an old trade. The place was now filled with shelves of toys, trinkets, and art supplies, stretching away into darkness.

"Light," Jalhan said, and Laokis lit a torch from a pack she carried upon her back. The room came into focus, and it was much the same as the rest of the buildings in town. It was empty. Not a thing out of place.

No … No, that wasn't true. The bear was gone, he knew that much already, but a series of iron poles stood bare at the front of the shop. Wooden puppets had been there, if he remembered correctly, life-sized and lifelike. They were gone now.

A clank of metal on stone filled the space, and Jalhan's sword came up as he crouched, on the defensive. Laokis pressed her back to his, her head turning quickly in either direction.

Clank. It came again. Closer. And then again. Closer and closer it came, the scrape of metal on stone, then a clank as whatever it was hit the floor again. It made itself known moments later, as the life-sized teddy bear approached. It was dragging a metal craftsman's hammer, the head dragging across the floor, before the bear raised it and slammed it down again.

The stuffed toy looked different. It was still tall, still fuzzy and brown, its eyes still glassy and haunting, but its outline seemed less defined. Misty droplets dripped from its eyes as though it were crying, and long, wispy claws speared from its paws, gripping the hammer tighter.

"Don't. Move." Jalhan whispered, his hand gripping the hilt of the borrowed sword tighter.

The bear made its shuffling way closer, the hammer bashing into a few items that had fallen off the shelves. They appeared to have been there a while, just the hazards of owning a business. Little wooden men lay scattered across the floor, and the weighty hamper promptly crushed one of them. Closer. Closer came the bear. Mist swirled up around the creature's feet, flowing up its body as if a suit of armor were forming around it. The hammer head grew spikes of mist that left gouges in the stone floor.

The bear was now only feet away, its eyes fixed on Jalhan. It raised the hammer. Jalhan raised his sword.

A wooden blur tackled the bear and the hammer

flew to the side, smashing into a shelf containing boxes of building blocks. Wooden bricks flew every which way. Jalhan rolled forward onto his knees while Laokis rolled to the side, dodging the flying debris. The wooden creature, one of the life-sized puppets, sat atop the bear, stabbing repeatedly down into it with a mist-covered whittling knife. Stuffing flew every which way, the color of blood, before puffing away into mist as it settled on the floor. Misty breath puffed from the creature's painted mouth, and it seemed to be humming something. A children's song that Jalhan knew well.

With a vicious downward slash, the puppet beheaded the stuffed bear, and a line of misty, cottony blood drifted away on an errant breeze. The puppet rose, collecting the bear's dropped hammer from the floor. By now, Jalhan and Laokis had rushed to the door, but found it had vanished, simply erased and replaced with a curtain of mist.

The puppet faced them, its expression locked in an eternal, phony smile. Its clothes, a fabric three-piece suit, were speckled with the bloody foam of the bear it had killed. Its strings writhed around it, lashing at the air with more force than should have been possible for such thin threads. As it approached, an army of little army men, porcelain and wooden dolls, and stuffed animals of all shapes and sizes approached, everything from dogs and cats to bears, lions, and tigers.

"Laokis," Jalhan said, as he drew his dagger into his left hand. "I wish we had known each other more."

"Aye," she said from beside him, waving her torch in one hand, her sword in the other. "As do I."

They waded forward into battle. Blades descended on Jalhan as various small knights and soldiers swarmed over his feet and ankles, finding the chinks in his leather boots. Needles of white-hot pain pierced his ankles and heel, and one of the mini-knights drove its large blade into Jalhan's calf. He ignored the pain, slashing, kicking, stomping. A porcelain doll rushed at him, a smaller hammer in its hand, and smashed it down on his big toe. Jalhan roared, kicked the doll hard and it flew away, shattering into bits of dripping porcelain on the floor.

Mist swirled through the battle, bolstering their foes. What would have been a simple poke became a horrible wound. A weak-looking stuffed cat drew a line of blood down Jalhan's face before his blade cut it in half. An ineffective tackle from a stuffed bear became a bull rush that knocked him onto his back.

Blades came from all sides. Claws. Teeth. The creatures delivered their blows with insane glee. They made no sound, however, and all he could hear was the rustle of cloth, the creaking of wood, the clank of metal, and the splatter of blood as a hammer bashed him in the nose, breaking it. Jalhan growled, lashing out with a dagger, his giant arms cutting a swath of destruction through the armies.

Flames surged around him as Laokis dove in with her torch. She'd been effective in her use of it, but she was soaked in blood just as he was. A nearly life-sized lion had cut her from her right eyebrow to the left corner of her mouth, and grotesque flaps of skin revealed bone beneath. Jalhan had to imagine he didn't look much better. They fought off the advances of the army of toys for what felt like hours. Days. But soon, just as suddenly as it had begun, the massacre was over. All that remained, standing like a general in the midst of his decimated army, was the puppet.

It clacked its hammer against its blade, head tilted in a teasing, mocking way. It stepped aside, revealing the remains of its brothers. Jalhan hadn't a clue how they'd gotten here, but the swirling mist around the puppet lurched about, and it was no longer a mystery to him. A face, wispy and gray, formed over the painted one, and a hollow voice, cold and distant, spoke a single phrase: "Too little."

The puppet lurched forward, and a pair of strings lashed out at Laokis and Jalhan. Despite their attempts to slash the tendrils aside, one raked across Jalhan's bicep, drawing blood through his leather jerkin. Blood splattered from Laokis as the string drove into her chest. She screamed as the string dragged her toward the puppet, her sword and torch dropping from nerveless fingers.

"No!" Jalhan cried, as the elf raised the hammer above its head.

It came down, shattering Jalhan's arm as he tried to block its force. Jalhan roared, his rage bubbling over like it hadn't in years. He started hacking, his sword blade biting deep, bloody holes into the wooden body of the creature. Little puffs of mist and splintery viscera flew, scoring his flesh and filling the air with a cloud of wispy red and grey. A second hammer blow came, and though it was only a glancing blow, he felt his ribs crack. He flew backward, smashing through the glass doors and out into the snow.

Jalhan rolled weakly in the snow, his mind only now processing the presence of the doors. He crawled weakly toward them, pulling a shard of glass from his thigh.

"Tirangil," he whispered. "Show mercy."

Jalhan felt a warm, golden glow about his body. He felt the touch of a hand, colder than ice, colder than anything he'd ever felt before, and that warmth turned to fire, scouring him of his wounds. Scouring him of his fatigue. Scouring him of all that sought to hold him back. But it was brief, and it was weaker than he had experienced in the past. But it was enough.

He leapt through the shattered door, charging into the misty interior. He picked up Laokis's guttering torch and roughly tackled the puppet off the slumped form of Laokis, who had a few new lacerations from the whittling knife the puppet held. With a savage growl, Jalhan shoved the torch into the puppet's face and it died, gargling mist, burning beneath him. He kicked the thing, which was blowing away to ash, and turned to heal Laokis.

The touch came again, and flowed from his hands into her beaten, nearly dead form. It revived her, just as it had him, but her wounds remained as slight, pink scars across her entire body. Something was not right here. Tirangil's mercy was stronger than this, and yet...

He helped a still-groggy and weak Laokis to her feet,

and the elf leaned against him, her long hair matted with blood and stuffing, and chips of wood and porcelain. The toy store was destroyed. Shelves had collapsed. Little fires licked at toy corpses in various places. Splinters of wood, porcelain, and broken scrap metal lay all about. But the mist had fled this place. It was done.

Night had fallen by the time they exited the toy shop, and the pair were far too tired to go on today. Jalhan felt his heart sink as they approached Laokis's home. They had achieved nothing that day. They had found a town devoid of life, infected by horrors neither of them understood. They had nearly failed. They had almost succumbed. And Halana was still gone.

All Jalhan could truly do as he wrestled with his own anger and regret was pray. He prayed to Tirangil. He begged the god for a miracle. He begged him for mercy. He begged the being to whom he'd dedicated his life for the past decade or more to give him guidance. But all he could feel was the fear, shaking him like the wind shook the trees of Sarvenkor outside.

As they lay in Laokis's bed, neither able to sleep, Jalhan reached across the space that separated them. She didn't pull away as he rested his hand on her back. He pulled her closer to him, holding her in his arms. He took comfort in her warmth, in the security that she was the one thing that was real in this forsaken place.

"We will find them," he said aloud, and he felt her nod against his chest.

He didn't tell her he had said that for his own benefit. He didn't let her see the lack of hope in his eyes.

Chapter Three

Kesa held her brother's hand as they shambled mindlessly through the tunnel. She distantly felt the need to protect the little boy, because her daddy had said so. When? She couldn't remember, but she would keep her promise. She was a princess, daddy had always said, and princesses protected their subjects. Little Jalhan, her brother, was her subject, and she would protect him.

That little spark of flame was a distant thing in her mind. All she could focus on was the mist. It was soothing. It was cool. It was grey. It reminded her of Mr. Pawsome, the once-brown stuffed bear she held ... No. No, Mr. Pawsome was gone. Left at home. That thought cut through the fog like a beam of sunlight, and Kesa began to cry, hot tears pouring down her cherubic face. She was here without her protector in this cold, damp place. She wished Uncle Jalhan was here. He'd know what to do. He'd protect her.

Her daddy stumbled just feet ahead of her. His step, normally bouncy, as Kesa liked to call it, was flat and shuffling. Her mother walked behind them. Kesa could sense her, shuffling along, her head down, as they descended far beneath the earth. Little Jalhan sniffled beside her, sensing the fear around him. Feeling the fear within him.

Kesa began to feel angry. Why was everything changing like this? Where were they? Why couldn't she stop?

The light in her mind began to grow. The mist began to retreat.

But all she could do was stumble onward.

***

The morning dawned cold and bleak, fitting for the first day of Aventir. The coldest month of the year was right on time, and even at mid-morning, it was damn near pitch black outside. Jalhan awoke, his body awash with aches and pains. Magical healing didn't remove the toll his wounds took on him, not entirely, and he could feel his body throbbing with its depleted energy. Laokis was gone, her spot on the bed now cold. She must have been up for a while, he guessed.

He went to the wash closet and did his business. He stood beneath the warm stream of water, a blessing in these larger villages, and let the sweat and dirt of the day before rush off him. It swirled away down the drain, and Jalhan watched it go, numbly.

He found Laokis, sitting quietly in her kitchen. She

held an earthenware mug between her delicate hands, but hadn't touched the coffee within it.

"Coffee's on," she said, her voice containing none of the playful edge it usually did. It was a flat, monotone thing, sounding of defeat and loss.

"Have you eaten?" Jalhan asked, as he poured the lukewarm coffee into a cup.

A fire smoldered in the fireplace, keeping the room just barely warm enough to be comfortable, but drafts of freezing air hit him every now and again. He seated himself across the pine log table, setting his cup down and ignoring it.

"No," Laokis responded, her eyes downcast. Her hands didn't move and her eyes didn't move up to meet his. She hid behind a curtain of unwashed hair and emotional barriers.

"You should," Jalhan said, as he finally picked up his mug, taking a sip. The bitter liquid shocked his system into wakefulness, and he drained the cup as though it were a tankard. "We've much to do today."

"Have we?" Laokis said, looking up for the first time since he'd walked in. "Have we much to do? Because if I really thought about it, really, I would say we'd just be heading out to play a fool's game. We'll walk through more buildings, see more unspeakable horrors, and find no progress forward."

Jalhan stared at her, stunned. Stunned by her outburst, yes, but ultimately stunned by just how much her sentiments mirrored his own. But the smiling face of Halana in his mind kept those thoughts at bay.

"Laokis," he began.

"Don't," she said, venom practically dripping from her lips. "You feel just the same as I do. I can see it in your face, in how you move. You cried last night, you know. You sobbed like the little scared boy you are, and I knew I couldn't trust you then."

"Laokis ..."

"And you continue to act like none of this matters to you. You're the high and mighty priest of Tirangil. Death doesn't scare you. If you lose those you love, you'll simply pray for their safety and wait to see them again in a few years. Hell, maybe you could see them now with your priestly gifts. You stand to lose nothing."

"Laokis!" he roared, his anger boiling over in a way it never did. The woman froze for a moment, rocking back in her chair. Jalhan's voice quieted to a near whisper as he leaned across the table toward her.

"Don't you think for one damn second that I have nothing to lose. I have everything to lose. I have a sister, a niece, a nephew, a brother-in-law who I abandoned for years because I was on some path of re-awakening. Some path of vengeance against the cruel world I was born into. I ignored their letters and their summons and their joyous occasions because a soldier of death needs none of those worldly comforts. Oh no, I was so much better. And now that I've discovered the error of my ways, the gods punish me. They take my sister from me. My family. And they leave me with a woman who would rather act as if she needs no one than admit that she's as afraid as everyone else is.

"You walked away from royalty and moved to a place like this, because you were afraid. Afraid of the responsibility you faced every day. So, you came here to free yourself of it all, and now that life has been taken away, and for the first time in decades, perhaps, you're being faced with responsibility again. And that scares you. I know all of that because that's exactly who I am. I came here with the intention to stay for a day and leave again. I have people expecting me back home. But the night I spent here, with you, with the villagers, taught me one thing: That this place is worth fighting for. I may feel hopeless now. I may feel as if we're fighting a losing battle. But dammit woman, it's a battle worth fighting, and I've had it with the self-pity. Throw all the stones you want. When that glass house breaks, you'll be all alone in the rubble with no one to save you."

He shoved his chair back and stood, turning toward the door. "I've a family to find."

Laokis said nothing as Jalhan moved away toward the door. She made no sound, made no move. Jalhan didn't care. He pulled on his boots, grabbed a fresh torch, but left the sword. He didn't need it. He didn't need her.

"Jalhan."

He froze. The voice was quiet. Raspy. So unlike Laokis, he was certain a mist demon had taken her place. He turned, slowly, to face her. Laokis sat there, her face blank, but her eyes pooled with tears. "I ... I'm sorry."

Jalhan didn't know what to say. It wasn't enough. It wasn't nearly enough. But he wouldn't put her through any more. It wasn't his place. She was struggling just as much as he was. Perhaps more. He simply nodded and turned toward the door again.

She joined him in his search an hour or so later, all evidence of their earlier fight gone. They wordlessly walked through another building, which was silent and cold, the ever-present mist keeping its distance. It wasn't until around midday that they made any progress. They stood in the center of town, looking across the snow-covered streets and buildings. A brief flash of sunlight broke through the mist and fog, and a building Jalhan had completely forgotten about made itself known.

"The temple," he said, and suddenly, his mind was awash with memories.

They had passed the temple on their way to the toy shop the day before and he had simply ignored it. He had passed over the slush and footprints of the passage of two hundred pairs of feet, but the temple's presence had simply slipped his mind.

"Dammit," he said, as Laokis echoed his sentiment. "You've seen it, too?"

"Yes," she said, turning toward the old stone building. "They're in there. I just know it."

Hope flared in Jalhan's chest for the first time in nearly two days. He hefted the borrowed sword, lit a fresh torch, and they made their way up the hill toward the great stone temple.

***

Kesa stood in a large room, so big her entire house could've fit in here. Her house. She wished she were there right now. She wanted to see Mr. Pawsome again.

She wanted to sit by the fire. She wanted a cookie. Mama made the best cookies. And cakes. Her mouth watered and she realized, for the first time in ... in ... she wasn't sure how long, she realized just how hungry she was. Her tummy rumbled, and the man in the black robe at the center of the room jerked his head up.

Kesa didn't like this man. He was tall, taller than Uncle Jalhan even, but skinny, like the baby tree behind her schoolhouse. Kesa liked that tree, but she didn't like this man. His head was shiny, hairless, and his face was constantly frowning, making it look pinched and ugly. His beady eyes were black, and the hands that emerged from the sleeves of his robes looked almost like bones.

"What was that?" he said in a nasally, nervous voice.

He sounded like what Kesa thought a rat might sound like. She wanted to laugh, but something kept her from it. She wanted to turn and leave, but she was rooted in place. The anger built up in her again, and she felt the grey blanket slipping ever further. She was still clutching little Jalhan's hand. Her hand was sweaty. She could see her brother out of the corner of her eye, and he stood, slack-jawed. The pain behind his eyes made Kesa angrier. The light in her mind grew as the man in the black robes went back to examining his hammer. All Kesa could hear were the sounds of labored breathing from the villagers all around her. She could smell the animals that had followed them down here. And all she could see was the rat man with the hammer. But the light began to grow.

Chapter Four

Although the footprints had been washed away in the past few days, Jalhan knew they were headed in the right direction. The stone façade of the temple was somehow out of place in this quaint little town, a tall, brooding structure of grey stone and high, stained-glass windows depicting the thirteen gods in various poses. That's how Jalhan remembered it, anyway, and it was mostly the same, though all of the windows, save those depicting Tirangil, had been smashed out. The front doors hung open slightly, banging shut and open again in the breeze. The mist was thick here, and as they approached, it swirled closer to them, forming into lashing chains that Jalhan narrowly avoided. Laokis took a scoring blow across her cheek, cursing as the mist retreated.

"I'm growing quite sick of all of this mist," Laokis growled, kicking at a patch of it that swirled about their feet. It solidified around her ankle and pulled her to her knees, and the elf woman drew her knife as if to cut off her own foot.

"Laokis, stop," Jalhan said calmly, taking her hand and pulling her to her feet. The mist relinquished its hold, and she shook herself, yanking her hand away from him as they climbed the steps of the temple.

"How can you be so calm?" she asked, and her façade of anger broke. She was trembling. She was being shown hope for the first time in days, and she was terrified that it would be stolen from her just as quickly.

"I'm not," he said, and meant it. "You just don't see

everything going on in my head."

Laokis grunted, and they approached the grand wooden double doors. Jalhan pushed them open with his sword, and they stepped into the cavernous interior. The place was a mess. Piles of shattered glass dotted the floor where the windows had been smashed in. The various altars to other gods had been burned, their statues toppled, paintings marred and slashed, tapestries torn down and desecrated. Only those that celebrated Tirangil remained, his angelic faces peering from one side of the room, his skeletal and demonic ones gazing from the other. Besides the broken effigies, there was not a person in sight. Snow had blown in and erased any tracks that may have been here. It came up to their ankles, crunching loudly in the echoic space.

"We search the floor," he said. "There may be old tunnel entrances here. A lot of these old churches had catacombs; this one should be no different."

Laokis said nothing and quietly moved away across the snowy carpet, her boots making no more sound on the snow as she moved. Jalhan, by comparison, sounded like a raging bull as he strode across the room. He dug at the snow with his sword, listening for any irregularities. He kicked over pews, moved destroyed artwork, and checked the walls for anything he could. It was all fruitless.

Laokis was moving much slower. She was focusing on things he never would have thought to look for such as air currents, which were harder to determine with the broken-out windows. Light changes. Sound. She was having as little luck as he was, starting in the center of the room and moving slowly outward.

After about an hour and a half, the answer came to them. Laokis was making a final pass around the edge of the room when she stopped. Polytheistic churches like this, Jalhan knew, always had one altar at the front of the church where any priest of any god was welcome to give praise. Jalhan had spoken at many of these in his time. He was never good at it, preferring to preach through action and example rather than words before a congregation. This church had one such altar, a great slab of wood with brass trimmings, sitting at the front center of the room. Laokis crouched before this now, listening. Watching. Then, Jalhan saw it. A strange breeze was blowing from the altar, raising swirling eddies of snow into the air.

"That's not coming from the window," Jalhan said, and the elf nodded dismissively.

"Help me," she said, rising, and began to push on the altar. Jalhan went to the other side, lifting and pulling. They had to break a bit of ice before the altar moved on well-oiled tracks, sliding back toward Jalhan. It revealed a staircase of worked marble, disappearing downward. The stench of humanity and livestock swirled up from below.

"We found them," Laokis breathed, her hands clutching the hilt of her longsword. "Jalhan, we ..."

Jalhan was already descending. His family was down there. His horse was down there. His sword was down there. And most of all, his target was down there. He hefted his torch and forged forward into the misty darkness.

The first mile of the stone corridor was the most frequently visited, Jalhan could tell. Worked stone, polished marble, now scuffed by the passage of feet and hooves and paws, and iron brackets with torches now burned down to the nub. Small alcoves, each filled with a gilded casket, lay on either side of the corridor, and Jalhan reflexively checked each one. They were all sealed. No misty undead would plague them ... he hoped.

The smell of old stone and iron was wholly masked by the stink of humanity: unwashed bodies, sweat, and breath. The scent of livestock was strong in the air, too, and was yet more powerful. They followed their noses. They followed the tracks. The marble and stone eventually gave way to dirt and rock. The alcoves became smaller, the coffins older and moldier, and the scent of damp earth mixed with the rest of the smells. All Jalhan could hear was the guttering torch, the rustle of cloth, and his and Laokis's breath as it steamed in the chill air.

They trudged onward, and the fervor of excitement wore off as they went. They had been walking for hours and had seen nothing; nothing other than the winding tracks of hundreds of pairs of feet.

The dirt and rock began to fade back into stone again, though this was of a more natural sort. The tunnels widened. The temperature dropped.

"Hold," Laokis said, her sharp eyes focused on a point on the ground. She crouched, and a moment later spoke. "Blood. Not much, and it's dried, but it's new. A day or two old."

She rose, and Jalhan followed in her wake. She paused every twenty yards or so, finding more droplets of blood. Soon enough, Jalhan was able to see it. They were footprints. The bloody footprints of people who had been walking far too long and at far too great a distance.

"We're close," she said. "Go slowly. We don't know what we'll be facing."

They fell into a crouch and Jalhan did his best to move quietly, though he was doing poorly. Laokis slipped ahead of him, a good thirty feet, and he let her. She would be able to stop him if it came to it. As it turned out, they had prepared far too early. They traveled another mile or so, but soon, they could hear it. The collective rumble of breath and the sound of livestock, coming from up ahead. It was still perhaps another half mile off – sound did move differently here – but they were close. Jalhan drew his sword again, keeping it close to his side as they moved forward. Laokis froze and Jalhan did, too, just a few inches behind her.

"Oh my gods," he breathed out, just as she did.

The entirety of Harban's Barrow stood in a great cavern about sixty feet in front of them. They could see them all there, standing in a ring around the great cavern, facing inward, unmoving. Standing just inside that circle, were the livestock, the pets, the animals. Dogs, cats, horses and cows stood side by side, making no sound, no motion, save the occasional snort or involuntary whimper. At the center of the room, facing away from them, stood a figure in a black robe, holding a pair of objects in his hands. He stood over a black pedestal, upon which sat a crystal that slowly pulsed, releasing puffs of mist into the air with each one. As the pair stood, the figure jerked upright, spinning to face them.

"No," he said, in a high-pitched, raspy voice. "No, no, this will not do."

He raised the objects in his hands, a hammer and a chisel, and smashed them together. The mist swirled about him, answering his commands, and a thick curtain of mist slammed into the cavern's archway, seemingly impenetrable. As Jalhan leaped toward it, the stone beneath his feet cracked and an iron hand burst its way through the floor. Thin cracks and lines and veins forked through the stone around them as misty fingers tore out veins of metal. The debris fell to the ground with a crash, and then began to move across the floor, dragged by the mist. The pieces were violently pulled and formed into a rough approximation of a human, with sharp, thin limbs and no head. It stood, shook itself, and then dropped to all fours, racing toward the pair.

"Go!" Laokis shouted, as she leapt effortlessly over the rushing creature, bringing her sword down upon it as she landed behind it. "I'll keep this thing busy. Get through the mist!"

Jalhan nodded. There was no time to question her. He turned and ran, flat out, toward the curtain of mist blocking him from his family. He dove forward, and the second his hands hit the mist, the world slowed. Sound faded. Sensations faded. All he felt was the mist. He stood in a gray void, swirling and silent. He stepped forward, and his boots walked across nothing at all. He made no sound. He wasn't falling. He wasn't rising. He could only move forward.

As he walked, he became aware of a presence in the fog with him. A cold presence, colder than anything he had ever known, yet somehow familiar. Jalhan knew who it was immediately.

"Lord Tirangil," Jalhan said, as he continued his walk. "Why have you done this?"

He received no response, but the towering, skeletal

figure made itself known, walking beside him, matching him step for step. Jalhan repeated his question.

"Why have you come here? Why have you done this? These are not sinners. These are not murderers and thieves. These are just people."

"I harvest souls where I must," the god of death rasped, his bones jittering as his voice boomed forth. "The souls of the innocent sate me in a way no others can."

"But you are merciful," Jalhan said, as he gripped his holy symbol. The golden skull with its silver halo was comforting in his hand, and the mist seemed to thin, just a bit. He thought he heard Laokis shouting at him from somewhere very, very far away.

"Mercy is weakness," the skeletal figure boomed, still walking beside Jalhan. "They approach me inevitably. What use is fifty more years of living?"

"What is fifty years to a god?" Jalhan asked.

Tirangil froze. Jalhan knew he had an advantage here. He mustn't waste it.

"The god of death is also the god of life. Without life,

you don't matter. Your mercy gives second chances. An afterlife is still a life, and you'd rather the people deserving of it burn while those who have lived righteously are given freedom."

"No," Tirangil said, though the word was a fleeting thing, weak and uncertain.

Jalhan raised his holy symbol and approached the towering, skeletal figure.

"You wish to save these people so they can live truly good lives, and that is less souls you must watch burn for all eternity. That eats you up inside, doesn't it, Lord Tirangil?"

"No!" the figure roared, as the mist swirled in around Jalhan, gripping his wrists, his elbows, his knees.

They yanked backward viciously, attempting to knock him off balance and drop the holy symbol. But even as his joints shattered and his vision blurred with pain, he clutched the golden skull in his hand.

"My lord," Jalhan wheezed, feeling more mist compress his ribs. "I pray for your mercy."

Just then, as he began to see blackness behind his eyes, a little hand reached into the mist and grabbed his. Suddenly, he was through the mist and lying flat on his back. His bones were unbroken. The pain was gone. He rolled onto his side and coughed, and a puff of the mist escaped his form, dispersing into the air as it rejoined the swirls of it spinning throughout the cavern. The curtain of mist had been broken, and he could see Laokis, still battling the bladed iron ore golem. He turned his head to see little Kesa, standing over him, her hands pressed to her mouth as she looked down at him in fear.

She took one away and whispered, fearfully, "Uncle Jalhan?"

His heart flooded with joy, and he sat up, hugging the little girl close as tears welled in his eyes.

"Kesa," he said, overwhelmed with emotion. "You've grown so big! You're a giant now!"

Kesa giggled, and Jalhan squeezed her all the tighter.

"How did you find us?" she said as Jalhan let her go.

"I searched and searched, and I guess Mr. Pawsome

knew exactly where to look."

Kesa's eyes widened.

"Mr. Pawsome told you?"

"Maybe," he said, taking her hand. "But I need you to do something for me. I need you to hide. See the lady in the hallway? Go to her when she's finished her task there. Stay with her. She'll protect you."

"But mama, and Jally—"

"—will be fine," he interrupted. "I'm here to save them. To save all of you. Now go."

Kesa walked uncertainly toward the hallway, but she felt comforted in seeing the beautiful elf and her sword. She ran down the hallway toward Laokis, just as the elf woman slashed the golem into fragments and they melted back into the stone.

Jalhan watched her go, then turned to face the priest, who was still performing whatever ceremony he'd been working on when Jalhan had slipped through the mist. He stood, now with his back to Jalhan, his voice rising and falling from a silent mouthing of words to barely above a whisper. This was no booming chant. This was a subtle, teasing cant that unnerved Jalhan. He could feel it in the air. The cold fingers of Lord Tirangil infecting every mind, freezing every soul. He felt blood running from his nose and, as he turned, he saw the villagers were under the same effect.

Jalhan brushed away the flecks of blood, moving closer to the priest. He squeezed between two horses, standing side by side, their heads drooped nearly to the floor. He reflexively patted their necks as he went, but they didn't react. They didn't even notice him. He had broken the circle. He walked, cautiously, toward the priest, his sword in hand, the hilt cold, nearly freezing. The temperature was dropping rapidly, and he could see his breath in the air in front of him. Somewhere, he heard the sound of a body collapsing, falling to the ground, succumbing to the cold. Then a second. Then a third. There was no other reaction from the crowd, just men and women falling dead, seemingly at random.

Jalhan had to act now. He had to stop this before his

sister, his family, were affected. He leaped forward and the priest spun faster than should have been possible, striking at Jalhan with his small hammer. Jalhan dodged and slashed at the priest, who slid away easily, his robes flaring with mist. Nearby, one of the two horses fell chest first to the floor, mist puffing from its eyes and ears as it died. Jalhan launched himself forward, punching the priest in the face with his empty hand as he brought his sword around. A hand, made entirely of grey mist, appeared from the priest's neck, catching the blade and wrenching it free of his hand. It spun away, hitting a bystander in the chest. The man didn't even react. He just stood there as blood poured down his front, creating a puddle around his feet.

The man standing beside the stricken one fell face first into the blood. Then a second, the dwarf who had been drinking beside Jalhan two nights, or an eternity ago, fell dead, dropping a loosely gripped tankard.

Jalhan drew his knife, his last defense. He stepped forward, slashing with the knife, but the hand appeared again. Jalhan was quicker this time, pulling the blade back as the mist tried to grasp it. He snap-kicked the priest between the legs, but felt as though he'd kicked a stone wall as the mist protected the pitiful creature.

"Lord Tirangil!" Jalhan shouted, as he rained ineffective blows upon the priest. "Show mercy! I beg you!"

The mist ... the Moranak, claimed another soul from somewhere in the room, and a great cloud of mist, swirling with the stolen souls, flowed into the priest.

Jalhan stabbed once more, but the mist caught the blade this time, and he felt the blade sink deep into his gut as the mist turned it back on him. He grunted, falling to his knees as he reached for the priest. Tendrils of the stuff grasped him by his limbs, wrapping around all of his extremities and holding him spread eagle against the ground. He watched as the priest raised his hammer, smashing it down upon the chisel in his other hand. A familiar sound came from somewhere in the room. A clop, like a horse's hoof. That's exactly what it was, and in a way he couldn't explain, he knew it was Bay, walking toward him. Shuffling. Zombielike.

"No," Jalhan murmured, his heart breaking. His horse was the closest thing he'd had to family while on the road, and he couldn't bear to think of the creature in that kind of pain. He heard the metal-shod hooves grow closer, closer. A shadow fell over him. The big horse stood above him, breathing steadily. He watched, helpless, as one of the huge hooves raised itself over his face.

"Bay," Jalhan said, and the hoof stopped. He watched as the horse shook itself, snorted, and raised its hoof again.

"Bay. Apple?"

The horse paused again, stepping back and stomping his hooves as he whinnied, shaking his head roughly.

The priest, mostly silent save for his continued chanting, smashed the chisel again, but Bay wasn't having it. He let out a mighty cry, rearing up and roughly kicking out at the priest. The mist immediately let Jalhan go free, and he rolled to the side as the muscled horse slammed down where he'd just been laying. The priest hadn't moved, having formed a shield of mist just in time, but Bay was livid.

The mighty horse paused, pawing at the ground like a charging bull might. Jalhan dove for the horse, pulling his greatsword from the saddle sheath, and stood beside his friend. He, too, was livid. He was tired of the mist. He was tired of the fear. He was tired of this rat-faced priest bastard and his stupid hammer. He was tired of being a pawn. Laokis leaped through the circle then, landing on the horse's other side, and Jalhan smiled over at her. Laokis smiled back. Whatever happened here today, this was going to end. Now.

Jalhan was the first to move. With a prayer to Tirangil's mercy on his lips, he stepped forward, slashing brutally down at the priest. Mist came up to block it, but Jalhan had expected that. Gripping his blade in both hands, he pushed forward as Bay kicked brutally at the priest's exposed midriff. Laokis circled behind him, slashing with sword and dagger, dodging tendrils of mist as she struck, faster than Jalhan could follow. Their attacks were all defeated by the mist, turned aside, and pushed back. But the duo wasn't stopping.

"Mercy," chanted Jalhan, as he struck and struck again. The Moranak was an active barrier to Tirangil's merciful side, the very manifestation of his evil on this earth. Jalhan had read plenty about it in his days, and he knew he just had to help the lord of death find his focus.

"Mercy!"

A hammer blow rang out through the room and the mist swirled anew. Jalhan struck at the rat-faced priest again, and he felt his sword hit something solid, like stone. Another villager died. Ten more. They had lost nearly fifty in the past four minutes, and Jalhan wouldn't let them lose anymore.

"Mercy!" he cried out, pushing forward with his blade. But to no avail. The mist swirled into a cyclone, grasping Bay by all four of his limbs and forcing the mighty beast to his knees.

Laokis was caught mid-leap, frozen there, hung by tendrils of mist gripping her limbs. She struggled, but the harder she did, the tighter the mist's grip grew. Jalhan heard a snap and a growl from Laokis as one of her arms shattered under the pressure.

Jalhan stood as the mist wrapped him like a constrictor snake. It squeezed, pushing his arms down. His sword tip hit the stone floor, but he did not let go, resisting the mist as best he could. A rib cracked. Then another. He could feel his forearms straining, muscles tearing, blood-vessels popping painfully. He was being crushed, and he knew it. But he kept to his mantra.

"Mercy ... Mercy ... Mercy ..."

Mercy came in the form of a little girl, her curls bouncing and her little fists pummeling. Kesa came rushing through the crowd of people, her little voice raised in a wordless cry of anger and fear. She rushed at the priest's legs, and as the man raised his hammer to strike her down, Jalhan felt it. The cold beginning to warm. The mist beginning to weaken. The light beginning to return. He felt Lord Tirangil's mercy.

With brutal efficiency, Jalhan broke free and strode

forward. He kicked the priest onto his back, and the hammer and chisel went flying in opposite directions. Jalhan seethed with rage, his eyes burning as he looked down upon the struggling, rat-faced man.

"Kesa," Jalhan said with eerie calm. "Cover your eyes."

The sword rose and fell, and the priest's head rolled. Jalhan stomped upon the corpse, which putrefied and crumbled before his very eyes, corrupted and torn asunder by the mist. Jalhan lifted his holy symbol, which was now glowing with white hot light, and the mist burned away as easily as if he'd focused the sun. It tried to flee, but he could feel it in a way he couldn't explain. He felt the mist screaming, crying out in fear and pain. Jalhan relished it. He felt the mist die, and he smiled. Mercy had been given to him, but he refused to return the favor.

As the mist faded, villagers all around the room began to awaken, coughing and spluttering, or finishing sentences they'd been speaking when the mist took effect. The confusion turned to fear, and screams began to fill the room.

"Calm!" Jalhan called above the ruckus, but nobody listened. Animals were beginning to rear and stampede, and Jalhan had to dodge as a raging bull charged toward him.

"CALM!" he boomed again, his holy symbol still in hand.

A white glow exploded from him, washing over the room, healing wounds and soothing emotions as it went. Jalhan fell to his knees as the power left him, feeling suddenly every bit of exhaustion. Laokis was there, catching and supporting him as he fell. He struggled back to his feet, leaning on her and his greatsword as he rose.

"Kesa," he called, looking to the little girl, who stood afraid nearby. He let his sword fall and limped over to her, crouching down to her as confusion again replaced the fear in the room. "Kesa, are you alright?"

"Yes," she said, strangely flatly. Her eyes were full of fear and trauma, and he knew she'd lost something today. They all had. He hugged the little girl as Halana, Hormas, and little Jalhan pushed through the crowd, surrounding them.

"Jalhan," Halana cried, hugging him as he rose to face her. "I thought you would ... I thought you had ..."

He hugged his sister back, tightly.

"We can talk about all of this later. We need to get everyone home. We need to mourn the dead. We need to rebuild."

"We?" Halana said, looking at him, strangely. "You'll be riding out first thing in the morning, won't you?"

Jalhan shook his head. "No. Not yet."

Halana nodded, tears of relief, joy, and sorrow pouring down her cheeks, which were gaunt and hollow after her days spent down here. The survivors left the tunnel system soon after. It took almost half a day to get everyone freed and returned to their homes. Healers and doctors ignored their own hunger and fatigue to care for the truly injured, and the undertaker moved about, blessing and shrouding the dead.

It wasn't until nearly a week later, on the seventh day of Aventir, that things began to calm. Rebuilding had begun in various places, and the old gnome toymaker was hard at work, rebuilding the toys he'd lost. Glassmakers had been called from Kuloran, and they would arrive next week to repair the damage done here. Jalhan had been hard at work, repairing damages of his own. He sat now with little Jalhan, reading to him from a book of stories the little boy had found on the bookshelf in the living room. It had a colorful cover, with a picture of a dragon on it, and Jally liked dragons. Jalhan did, too.

"Have you ever seen one, Uncle?" asked the little boy, who had taken the events of the previous week surprisingly well.

"Not yet," Jalhan said. "I hope to one day. Maybe we can go on a dragon discovering adventure together when you grow up."

Jally's eyes widened in excitement, and he jumped up, cheering and clapping.

"You can go discover dragons tomorrow," Halana said as she walked in. "Go wash up for supper."

Jally groaned with annoyance, but did as he was told.

He already knew better than to test his mother. Jalhan stood to follow, but Halana called him back. "We should talk," she said as he sat back down on the sofa.

"Alright," Jalhan said. "What about?"

"You're leaving again, aren't you?"

Jalhan nodded. There was no fooling Halana.

"Tomorrow."

"Where?" she asked him.

"Moralon Etherhal."

Halana gasped. She hadn't been expecting that one.

"That cursed place? But why?"

"Answers," Jalhan said.

"Answers to what?"

"I don't know yet. But I can feel it there, Hally. I can feel the mist just on the other side of those trees. It's miles, hundreds of miles away, and I can still feel it."

Halana nodded.

"I believe you. We were possessed by the mist, but you …"

She trailed off. She didn't have to tell him.

"I'll join you for dinner tonight," he said. "I'll tuck in my niece and nephew. I'll have a drink with Hormas. But in the morning, I'm leaving."

Halana nodded. She knew better than to try and stop him. She wouldn't have tried even if she could. "Then we'll make the most of it."

Jalhan spent the evening in the company of family. He laughed at Hormas's dirty jokes over fine, aged whiskey. He played jokes on Kesa and Jally over the dinner table, much to Halana's chagrin. He reminisced with stories of their younger days with Halana, laughing at the humorous, sharing moments of melancholy silence for the sad. It was a night for repairing rifts done by years on the road. It was healing.

The next morning, he left before light. He carried his pack over one shoulder, and he had a pouch of coins ready for the stable master. He heard footsteps crunching through the fresh snow as he approached the stable. It was Laokis. She was dressed similarly to him, and she carried her bow in an oiled leather tube under one arm.

"You're sure you feel it, too?" he asked her as they walked, side by side.

"I'm quite sure, Jalhan. Are you?"

He chuckled. "I think the tugging of a god's essence is quite noticeable, don't you?"

She grunted, but let out a small laugh in response. They entered the stables, paid the owner, and left the village of Harban's Barrow as the light's first rays touched the sky. They turned east and north, angling inland away from the sea, and set forth on their journey.

Jalhan looked back at the small village behind him. He watched as puffs of smoke began to fill the air as breakfast fires were relit.

"I'll return," he promised, then kicked Bay into a trot to catch up with Laokis. With his heart full, he rode toward a future touched by mist.

Acknowledgements

You may think that a short story is nothing special. It's a fraction of a novel, a story that starts and finishes in the span of a brief read. But this story would not even exist today if it weren't for some very important people and their ability to drive me forward.

I'd like to begin by thanking Mason Armstrong, and later, Colton Hill, for their invention and management of Sketchbook: Your World, respectively. Without you two, I'm not sure Kirandur would have ever existed, or it would have taken far longer to do so.

I'd like to thank my frequent collaborative partner, Lauren Celeste, for helping me fill out all those NPC's on the game that started it all, and giving me ideas and inspirations for new places and people. Thank you for believing in it, in me, and helping me fill it out in places that looked pretty empty of people.

I'd like to thank The Byte Bender for believing in me enough to help me realize my vision of making an audio MMO. It's happening! It's really happening! I can't wait until it's in my hands and everyone else's. He really is a wizard, and his help has been invaluable. Thank you for making my dream come true.

I'd like to thank Oscar Ramirez for being one of the staunchest supporters of Kirandur. He's even tried to write his own in world lore for some of his characters, and that just absolutely thrills me. I mean, how cool is it that I've already got fan fiction! I'm incorporating some of it into cannon, but all the same!

I'd like to thank some of my closest friends, Ryan Roles, Luis Villa-Lozano, and Zechariah Benoit. You turned my city guard captain into Raymond Holt, and he'll never show up again, probably, maybe, but it was legendary, and it made me feel that you cared about my world. It's going to only grow, and I look forward to the shenanigans we get up to in that. This thank you goes to my entire D&D group. Even if I did not mention your name here, know that you're just as important and I love you all.

I'd like to thank my team over at The Kuloran Players. From design work to writing, you've all given me the inspiration to do better and work harder. Without you, this game we're making together would be a huge mess design-wise. You help ground me, but also push my vision forward. You play to my inner passions and that means the world to me.

I'd like to thank Malia Suhr, Jacquelyn, and Cheyenne Raine, my three beta readers, for helping me iron things out. The reason this story actually looks good is because of them. I don't say that lightly, either. They actually do so much of the heavy lifting when it comes to correcting me. Thank you all, you're invaluable to me.

I'd be remiss if I didn't also thank my editor and publisher, Mike Dauplaise at M&B Global Solutions Inc. Publishing a book has been my dream for many years, and it's now being realized thanks to your help. Seriously, the gravity of this is not lost on me, and this opportunity is one I'll treasure forever. As I write this, I am giddily awaiting the day I can hold the paperback in my hands. Your work and passion for the craft has made this experience a breeze, and I know my book is going to look and feel great. Thank you, again, so much. You've changed my life and I can't stress that enough.

I'd like to give thanks to my friends in Sigma Tau Delta, the English Honors Society. You are a group of kindred spirits who showed me such love and enthusiasm when I told you all this was coming out. I can't wait for you all to read it, and I can't wait to grow and thrive with you. Seriously, you guys are my people. I found my people on this campus and I didn't think that would happen this go around.

I'd like to thank Allan Jamir, my mentor and close friend, for introducing me to my publisher, Mike. Without him connecting us, this book would not have become reality. Beyond that, though, he has been the driving force behind my go-get-it attitude and ability to network, and he's just made me a better person. My life is better for having had you in it, Al. Thank you for all you've done for me.

But my most special thanks goes out to the player base of Sketchbook: Your World. You've seen Kirandur grow from a single map into ... whatever you want to call it now. A world? A universe? I call it my happy place, and because of you all, it's grown and changed and matured into something I can be truly proud of. Thank you all for your support, and I hope I'll have it for years to come.

There are countless other names I'm missing. My

sister, Abby, and her wife, Sara. My mother, my father, my younger brother, and Nash, of course. (He's my dog. Can't forget him.) There are too many people for me to thank here. There are too many beers I owe, too many thanks I haven't given. But just know, all of you, that even though this published project you're reading now is short and, hopefully, sweet, the effort it took to get here was monumental. And I couldn't have done it without you.

With love,
Baylee

About the Author

Baylee Alger is a Wisconsin-based fantasy writer who spends a great deal of time imagining and writing new stories in his world of Kirandur. Baylee went blind at the age of two due to brain cancer, and has used his lack of sight to foster a vibrant imagination, brimming with story ideas and characters to fill them. He is a college student, and hopes one day to become a successful journalist as well as author. He spends a great deal of time thinking up new story ideas, playing Dungeons & Dragons with his best friends, and being with his guide dog, Nash.

www.ingramcontent.com/pod-product-compliance
Lightning Source LLC
Chambersburg PA
CBHW051711180726
48283CB00004B/1298